I LOVE MY SHADOW!

by Hans Wilhelm

Hello Reader! — Level 1

P9-ELR-602

SCHOLASTIC INC.

Cartwheel
B·O·O·K·S®

New York   Toronto   London   Auckland   Sydney   Mexico City   New Delhi   Hong Kong

I am going to the beach.

Look!
I brought a friend.

I like to chase him.

But sometimes
he chases me.

He can be short and fat.

But sometimes
he is very tall and thin.

My friend can be
very funny.

And sometimes he can be
a little scary.

But he always likes
to play with me.

Oh, no!
Here comes
a big cloud.

Now my friend
is gone.

I am all alone.

I know what to do!

I chase the cloud away!

Now my friend is back again.

We are a great team.